# Pete the Cat and His Four Groovy Buttons

# Pete the Cat

# Four Groovy Buttons

Written by
Eric Litwin
Art by
James Dean
(creator of Pete the Cat)

SCHOLASTIC INC.

ISBN 978-0-545-64914-8



12 11 10 9 8 7 6 5 16 17 18/0

Printed in the U.S.A. 40

First Scholastic printing, September 2013

Typography by Jeanne L. Hogle

To Trey and Destiny
Always be honest, give more than you take,
and follow your dreams.
—J.D.

To Zelda Litwin, my mother,
whose creative spirit nurtured my imagination.
—E.L.

Pete the Cat put on his favorite shirt with four big, colorful, round, groovy buttons.

He loved his buttons so much, he sang this song:

4

"My buttons, my buttons,
my four groovy buttons.
My buttons, my buttons,
my four groovy buttons."

One of the buttons popped off
and rolled away.

How many buttons are left?

THREE
3
4-1=3

3
groovy!

Did Pete cry?
Goodness, no!
Buttons come and buttons go.

He kept on singing his song:

"My buttons, my buttons,
my three groovy buttons.
My buttons, my buttons,
my three groovy buttons."

POP!

OH NO!

Another button popped off and rolled away!

How many buttons are left?

TWO
2
3-1=2

Did Pete cry?
Goodness, no!

Buttons come and
buttons go.

He kept on singing his song:

"My buttons, my buttons,
my two groovy buttons.
My buttons, my buttons,
my two groovy buttons."

ICE CREAM

POP!

OH NO!

Another button popped off and rolled away!

How many buttons are left?

ONE
1
2-1=1

Did Pete cry?
Goodness, no!

Buttons come and buttons go.

He kept on singing his song:

"My button, my button,
my one groovy button.
My button, my button,
my one groovy button."

POP!

OH NO!

The last button popped off and rolled away!

How many buttons are left?

ZERO
0
1-1=0

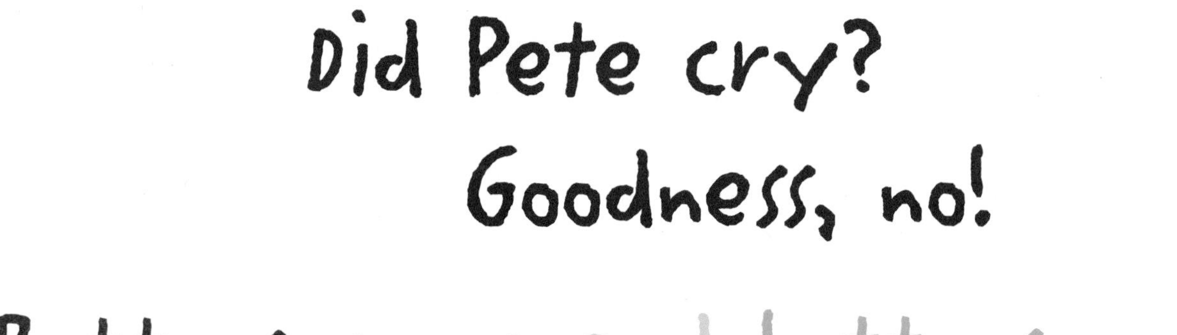
Did Pete cry?
Goodness, no!

Buttons come and buttons go.

Pete looked down at his buttonless shirt,
and what do you think he saw?

# HIS BELLY BUTTON!

And he kept on singing his song:

IT'S ALL GOOD!

"My button, my button,
still have my **belly button.**
My button, my button,
still have my **belly button.**"

I guess it simply goes to show that stuff will come and stuff will go.

**But do we cry?**

**Goodness, NO!**

We keep on singing.

Buttons come and buttons go.

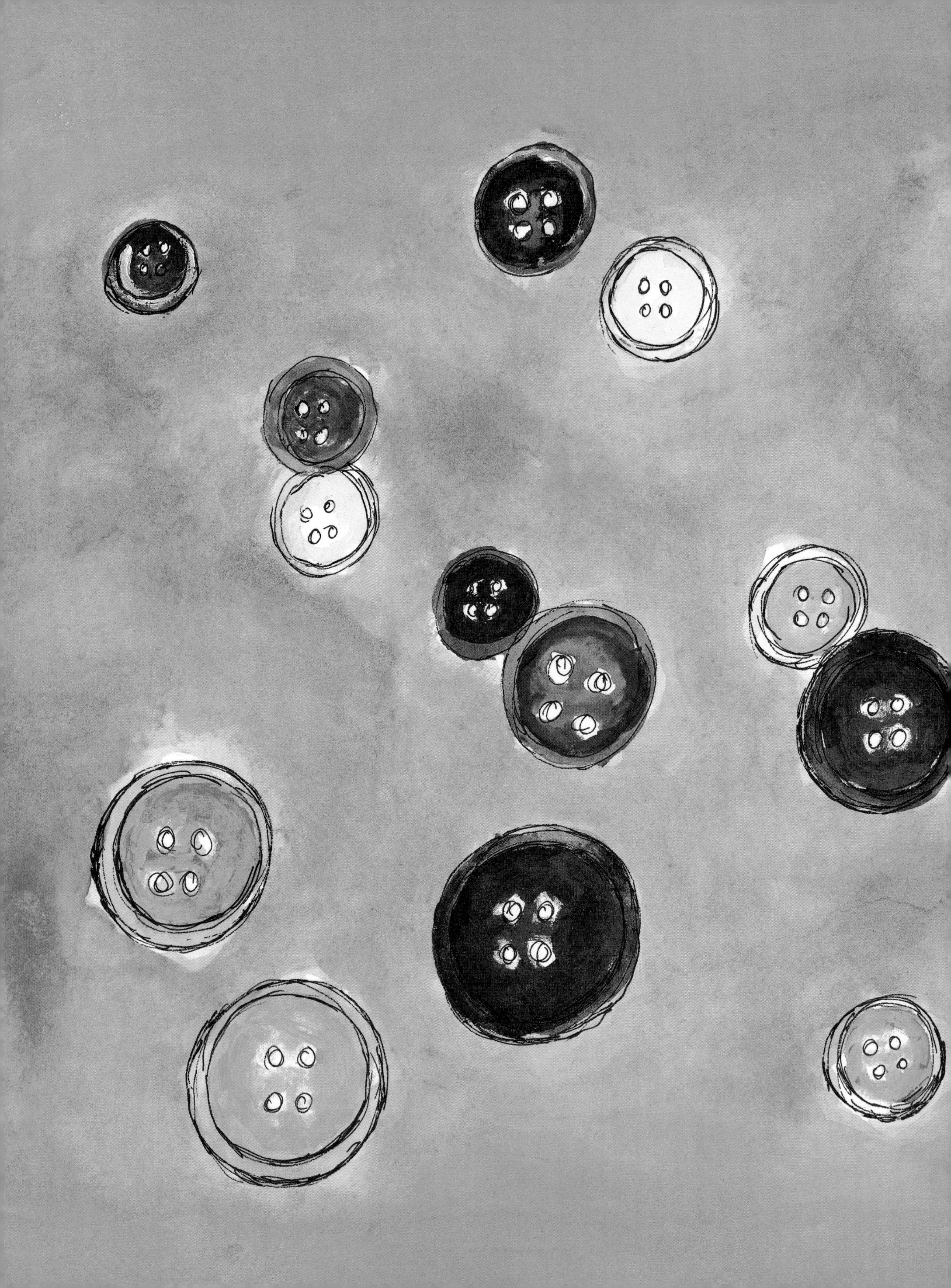